Dark Man

How many

Second series

First series

Dark Man

The Dark Words
by Peter Lancett
illustrated by Jan Pedroietta

Published by Ransom Publishing Ltd.
51 Southgate Street, Winchester, Hants. SO23 9EH
www.ransom.co.uk

ISBN   978 184167 602 9

First published in 2007
Second printing 2008

A CIP catalogue record of this book is available from the British Library.

The rights of Peter Lancett to be identified as the author and of Jan
Pedroietta to be identified as the illustrator of this Work have been
asserted by them in accordance with sections 77 and 78 of the
Copyright, Design and Patents Act 1988.

David Strachan, The Old Man, and The Shadow Masters appear by
kind permission of Peter Lancett.

Dark Man

The Dark
Words

by Peter Lancett

illustrated by Jan Pedroietta

Ransom

Chapter One:
Magical Words

The Dark Man sits against the bare bricks of a wall.

He is in a ruined shop.

The sun shines through a hole in the roof.

The Dark Man wants to sleep, but he cannot.

Suddenly, he feels that he is not alone.

He opens his eyes to see the Old Man standing before him.

"You do not look well," the Old Man says.

"I am very tired," the Dark Man replies.

The Old Man nods slowly.

"I want you to leave the city tonight," he says.

"An old document, that has been lost for many years, has been discovered. It is deep in the forest. It must not fall into the wrong hands."

"Why is it so important?" the Dark Man asks.

"The words on the document are magical," the Old Man says. "They are very powerful."

Later, the Dark Man is walking through the forest.

It is night and he is walking far from the path.

The Dark Man has not been in a forest for a long time.

Many years ago, forests were like a second home to him.

He has not forgotten how to move in the forest. Dead leaves cover the ground, but the Dark Man moves in silence.

Chapter Two:
Little Boys Like to Play

A sound comes from his left.

The Dark Man stops and looks.

A shadow darts through the trees. The Dark Man keeps still.

Slowly, a head appears from behind a tree.

"Show yourself," the Dark Man says.

A small boy steps into the open.

"Come over here," the Dark Man says. "Don't be afraid."

The small boy starts to walk slowly. His feet crunch on the leaves.

The boy is dressed in rags and he is very dirty.

"Who are you?" the boy asks.

"I am from the city," the Dark Man tells him. "Who are you?"

The boy shrugs.

"I live here," he says. "In the forest."

"Where are your parents?" the Dark Man asks.

"I don't remember," the boy replies. "I have always lived in the forest."

"The forest is not safe," the Dark Man says.

The boy shrugs again. "Why are you here at night?" he asks.

"Something is hidden here," the Dark Man tells him.

"The secret paper?" the boy asks. "I know where it is. I can take you to it."

The Dark Man nods. "That would save me time."

He reaches to take the boy's hand, but the
boy pulls his arm away and steps back.

The Dark Man shrugs.

"Lead on," he says.

The boy goes deep into the forest.

The Dark Man follows and notices that now the boy moves silently.

He too does not crunch the leaves or twigs.

Sometimes, the boy runs so far ahead that the Dark Man cannot see him.

Then the Dark Man waits for the boy to show himself.

The boy is playing, and the Dark Man does not mind. He knows that little boys like to play.

Suddenly, the boy slows down.

"Are we close to the secret paper?" the Dark Man asks.

The boy turns and his face is stern.

"Quiet," he says. "The secret paper is not far, but there is something else."

Chapter Three:
She Never Moves

The little boy turns and points.

There is someone sitting at the base of a tree. It is a young woman.

She sits very still.

The Dark Man can see that her eyes are open. But she does not seem to see anything. She simply stares ahead.

The little boy moves past her.

He beckons the Dark Man to join him. The Dark Man steps carefully past the girl.

"Who is she?" the Dark Man asks.

"I don't know," the boy replies. "She has been sitting there for two days. She never moves."

The boy goes deeper into the forest. The Dark Man follows.

They walk for more than an hour. Then the boy stops again.

The Dark Man looks over the boy's shoulder.

They are back with the sitting girl. They have walked in a circle.

"What is going on?" the Dark Man asks.

The boy giggles. He turns to step past the sitting girl, but he trips. He puts his hands out, as he tumbles onto her lap.

The Dark Man is startled by what he sees.

As the boy's hands make contact with the girl, his hands and his arms become dust.

The boy seems to fall right through the girl, until he is rolling on the ground next to her.

The dust has re-formed. It has become the little boy again.

Now the Dark Man knows that there is something magical about the boy.

And the girl, too.

Chapter Four:
"Free Us"

The girl turns her head to look at the boy.

Beams of bright light erupt from her eyes, passing through the boy, and he screams.

The light beams illuminate a large hole in the base of a nearby tree.

The Dark Man can see into the hole.

Inside, there is a large scroll. It is the old document.

He rushes over to collect it.

The boy screams and tries to stop him.

The boy's hands turn to dust again as he tries to grab the Dark Man.

The Dark Man starts to unroll the document.

"No!" a voice cries.

The Dark Man turns to the girl.

"Do not read it. You will become like us."

The words come from the girl, but her mouth does not move.

"Just read the words along the outside of the scroll. Free us."

The Dark Man looks at the scroll and sees words that he does not understand.

He reads them out loud.

A strong wind knocks him to the ground.

He turns and sees the boy and the girl turn to dust. They are both screaming.

Then they are carried away on the strong wind.

The Dark Man hears a sigh, and a soft voice that says,

"Thank you."

The Dark Man tucks the document inside his coat. He turns to head back to the city.

He will have to ask the Old Man about the boy and the girl.

The author

photograph: Rachel Ottewill

Peter Lancett is a writer, fiction editor and film maker, living and working in New Zealand and sometimes Los Angeles. He claims that one day he'll 'settle down and get a proper job'.